Magic Tree House® Books

#1: Dinosaurs Before Dark
#2: The Knight at Dawn
#3: Mummies in the Morning
#4: Pirates Past Noon
#5: Night of the Ninjas
#6: Afternoon on the Amazon
#7: Sunset of the Sabertooth
#8: Midnight on the Moon
#9: Dolphins at Daybreak
#10: Ghost Town at Sundown
#11: Lions at Lunchtime
#12: Polar Bears Past Bedtime
#13: Vacation Under the Volcano
#14: Day of the Dragon King
#15: Viking Ships at Sunrise
#16: Hour of the Olympics
#17: Tonight on the *Titanic*
#18: Buffalo Before Breakfast
#19: Tigers at Twilight
#20: Dingoes at Dinnertime
#21: Civil War on Sunday
#22: Revolutionary War
    on Wednesday
#23: Twister on Tuesday
#24: Earthquake in the
    Early Morning
#25: Stage Fright on a
    Summer Night
#26: Good Morning, Gorillas
#27: Thanksgiving on Thursday
#28: High Tide in Hawaii

Merlin Missions

#29: Christmas in Camelot
#30: Haunted Castle on Hallows Eve
#31: Summer of the Sea Serpent
#32: Winter of the Ice Wizard
#33: Carnival at Candlelight
#34: Season of the Sandstorms
#35: Night of the New Magicians
#36: Blizzard of the Blue Moon
#37: Dragon of the Red Dawn
#38: Monday with a Mad Genius
#39: Dark Day in the Deep Sea
#40: Eve of the Emperor Penguin
#41: Moonlight on the Magic Flute
#42: A Good Night for Ghosts
#43: Leprechaun in Late Winter
#44: A Ghost Tale for Christmas Time

#45: A Crazy Day with Cobras
#46: Dogs in the Dead of Night
#47: Abe Lincoln at Last!
#48: A Perfect Time for Pandas
#49: Stallion by Starlight
#50: Hurry Up, Houdini!
#51: High Time for Heroes
#52: Soccer on Sunday

Magic Tree House® Fact Trackers

Dinosaurs
Knights and Castles
Mummies and Pyramids
Pirates
Rain Forests
Space
Titanic
Twisters and Other Terrible Storms
Dolphins and Sharks
Ancient Greece and the Olympics
American Revolution
Sabertooths and the Ice Age
Pilgrims
Ancient Rome and Pompeii
Tsunamis and Other Natural Disasters
Polar Bears and the Arctic
Sea Monsters
Penguins and Antarctica
Leonardo da Vinci
Ghosts
Leprechauns and Irish Folklore
Rags and Riches: Kids in the Time of
    Charles Dickens
Snakes and Other Reptiles
Dog Heroes
Abraham Lincoln
Pandas and Other Endangered Species
Horse Heroes
Heroes for All Times
Soccer

Magic Tree House® Activity Books

Games and Puzzles from the Tree House
Magic Tricks from the Tree House
My Magic Tree House Journal
Magic Tree House Survival Guide

MAGIC TREE HOUSE® #3
Full-Color Edition

Mummies

in the *Morning*

by Mary Pope Osborne

illustrated by Sal Murdocca

A STEPPING STONE BOOK™

Random House New York

Text copyright © 1993, 2014 by Mary Pope Osborne
Jacket art and interior illustrations copyright © 1993, 2014 by Sal Murdocca

All rights reserved. Published in the United States by Random House Children's Books, a division of Random House LLC, a Penguin Random House Company, New York. Originally published in a different form by Random House Children's Books, New York, in 1993.

Random House and the colophon are registered trademarks and A Stepping Stone Book and the colophon are trademarks of Random House LLC. Magic Tree House is a registered trademark of Mary Pope Osborne; used under license.

Visit us on the Web!
MagicTreeHouse.com
randomhouse.com/kids

Educators and librarians, for a variety of teaching tools, visit us at
RHTeachersLibrarians.com

Library of Congress Cataloging-in-Publication Data
Osborne, Mary Pope.
Mummies in the morning / Mary Pope Osborne ; illustrated by Sal Murdocca. —
First full-color edition.
pages cm. — (Magic tree house ; #3)
Originally published in a different form by Random House Children's Books,
New York, in 1993.
Summary: Jack and his younger sister take a trip in their tree house back to ancient Egypt, where they help a queen's mummy continue her voyage to the Next Life.
ISBN 978-0-385-38758-3 (trade) — ISBN 978-0-385-38759-0 (lib. bdg.) —
ISBN 978-0-385-38760-6 (ebook)
[1. Time travel—Fiction. 2. Mummies—Fiction. 3. Kings, queens, rulers, etc.—
Fiction. 4. Ghosts—Fiction. 5. Magic—Fiction. 6. Tree houses—Fiction.
7. Egypt—History—332–30 B.C.—Fiction.] I. Murdocca, Sal, illustrator. II. Title.
PZ7.O81167Mr 2014 [Fic]—dc23 2013039575

MANUFACTURED IN CHINA

10 9 8 7 6 5 4 3 2 1

First Full-Color Edition

For Patrick Robbins,
who loves ancient Egypt

Dear Readers,

Kids often ask me where I get my ideas for Magic Tree House books. And I often answer, "From readers like you!" Ever since I started writing the series over twenty years ago, kids have been giving me great suggestions of where Jack and Annie should go in the tree house. Whenever I visit schools or bookstores, my audience votes on the different ideas I'm thinking about.

That's how I discovered that many readers have a great interest in the civilization of ancient Egypt. Ancient Egypt had always seemed like a very mysterious and exciting place to me, too. But before I could write about it, I had to do a lot of research. I read books about pyramids built almost 5,000 years ago and the mummies buried inside. I learned about the strange beliefs surrounding the burial of Egyptian pharaohs and queens. I learned about tomb treasure and tomb robbers.

I hope you will find all these subjects as amazing as I did when I worked on *Mummies in the Morning*. If you want to learn even more about ancient Egypt, check out the Magic Tree House Fact Tracker *Mummies and Pyramids*, written by my husband, Will Osborne. This nonfiction companion to *Mummies in the Morning* tells you all the facts behind Jack and Annie's fictional Egyptian adventure.

Today, Will and I feel as if we both actually traveled to ancient Egypt. When we wrote our books, we used our imaginations to slip out of our normal lives and into another world. We felt the hot desert winds. We smelled the musty odor inside a pyramid. We admired the gleaming beauty of the golden treasures.

Reading a book is a lot like writing a book. You are about to slip out of your everyday world and travel with Jack and Annie to the world of ancient Egypt. I hope you'll have a wonderful adventure. It might be a little scary, but after your morning with mummies, I promise you'll be back home in time for lunch!

Mary Pope Osborne

Contents

CHAPTER ONE

MEOW!

"It's still here," said Jack.

"It looks empty," said Annie.

Jack and his seven-year-old sister gazed up at a very tall oak tree. At the top of the tree was a tree house.

Late-morning sunlight lit the woods. It was almost time for lunch.

"Shhh!" said Jack. "What was that noise?"

"What noise?"

"I heard a noise," Jack said. He looked

around. "It sounded like someone coughing."

"I didn't hear anything," said Annie. "Come on. Let's go up." She grabbed the rope ladder and started climbing.

Jack tiptoed over to a clump of bushes. He pushed aside a small branch.

"Hello?" he said. "Anybody there?"

There was no answer.

"Jack! Come on!" Annie called down. "The tree house looks the same as it did yesterday."

Jack still felt that someone was nearby. Could it be the person who'd put all the books in the tree house?

"Ja-ack!" called Annie.

Jack gazed over the top of the bushes.

Was the mysterious M person watching him now? Maybe M wanted the gold medallion back—the one Jack had found on their dinosaur adventure. Maybe M wanted the leather bookmark back—the one from the castle book.

There was an M on the medallion and an M on the bookmark. But what did M stand for?

"Tomorrow I'll bring everything back," Jack said loudly.

A breeze swept through the woods. The leaves rattled.

"Come on!" called Annie.

Jack went back to the big oak tree. He grabbed the rope ladder and climbed up.

When he reached the top, he crawled through a hole in the wooden floor. He tossed down his backpack and pushed his glasses into place.

"Hmmm. Which book is it going to be today?" said Annie. She was looking at the books scattered around the tree house.

Annie picked up the book about castles. Just yesterday, the castle book had taken Jack and Annie back to the time of knights.

"Hey, this isn't wet anymore," she said. She handed the book to Jack.

"You're right!" said Jack, amazed. The book had gotten soaked in a castle moat, but today it looked fine. Jack silently thanked the mysterious knight who had rescued them.

"Watch out!" warned Annie. She waved a dinosaur book in Jack's face.

"Put that away," Jack said nervously. The day before yesterday, the dinosaur book had taken them to the time of dinosaurs. Jack silently thanked the Pteranodon who had saved him from a Tyrannosaurus rex.

Annie put the dinosaur book back with the other books. Then she gasped.

"Wow," she whispered. "Look at *this*." She held up a book about ancient Egypt.

Jack caught his breath. He took the book from her. A green silk bookmark was sticking out from between the pages.

Jack turned to the page with the bookmark. There was a picture of a pyramid.

Going toward the pyramid was a long parade. Four huge cows with horns were pull ing a sled. On the sled was a long gold box. Many Egyptians were walking behind the sled. At the end of the parade was a sleek black cat.

"Let's go there," whispered Annie. "Now."

"Wait," said Jack. He wanted to study the book a bit more.

"Pyramids, Jack," said Annie. "You love pyramids."

It was true. Pyramids *were* high on Jack's list of favorite things, after knights and dinosaurs—*plant-eating* dinosaurs, that is.

He didn't have to worry about being eaten by a pyramid.

"Okay," he said. "But hold the Pennsylvania

book. In case we want to come right back here."

Annie found the book with the picture of their hometown in it: Frog Creek, Pennsylvania.

Jack pointed to the pyramid picture in the Egypt book. He cleared his throat and said, "I wish we could go to this place."

"*Meow!*"

"What was *that*?" Jack looked out the tree house window.

A black cat was sitting on a branch right outside the window. The cat was staring at Jack and Annie.

It was the strangest cat Jack had ever seen. It was very sleek and dark, with bright yellow eyes and a wide gold collar.

"It's the cat in the Egypt book," whispered Annie.

The wind started to blow. The leaves began to shake.

"Here we go!" cried Annie.

The wind whistled louder. The leaves shook harder.

Jack closed his eyes as the tree house started to spin.

It spun faster and faster.

Then everything was still.

Absolutely still.

CHAPTER TWO

OH, MAN. MUMMIES!

"*Meow!*"

Jack and Annie looked out the window.

The tree house was perched on the top of a palm tree. The tree stood with about a dozen other palm trees. They were in a patch of green surrounded by a desert.

"*Meow!*"

Jack and Annie looked down.

The black cat was sitting at the bottom of the tree. The cat's yellow eyes were staring up at Jack and Annie.

"Hi!" Annie shouted.

"Shhh," said Jack. "Someone might hear you."

"In the middle of a desert?" said Annie.

The black cat stood up and began walking around the tree.

"Come back!" Annie called. She leaned out the window to see where the cat was going.

"Oh, wow!" she said. "Look, Jack."

Jack leaned forward and looked down.

The cat was running away from the palm trees toward a giant pyramid in the desert.

A parade was going toward the pyramid. It looked exactly like the parade in the Egypt book.

"It's the picture from the book!" said Jack.

"What are those people doing?" asked Annie.

Jack looked down at the Egypt book. He read the words under the picture:

> **When a royal person died, a grand**
> **funeral procession took place.**
> **Family, servants, and other mourners**
> **followed the coffin. The coffin was**
> **called a sarcophagus. It was pulled on**
> **a sled by four oxen.**

"It's an Egyptian funeral," said Jack. "The box is called a sar . . . sar . . . sar . . . oh, forget it." He looked out the window again.

The oxen, the sled, the Egyptians, and the black cat were all moving in a slow, dreamy way.

"I'd better make some notes about this," said Jack.

Jack liked to make notes. He reached into his backpack and pulled out his notebook. Jack wrote:

coffin called sarcophagus

"We'd better hurry," said Annie, "if we want to see the mummy."

Annie started down the rope ladder.

Jack looked up from his notebook.

"Mummy?" he said.

"There's probably a mummy in that gold box," Annie called up. "We're in ancient Egypt. Remember?"

Jack loved mummies. He put down his pencil.

"Good-bye, Jack!" called Annie.

"Wait!" Jack called.

"Mummies!" Annie shouted.

"Oh, man," said Jack. "Mummies!"

Jack shoved his notebook and the Egypt book into his pack. Then he started down the ladder.

When Jack got to the ground, he and Annie took off across the sand.

As they ran, a strange thing happened. The closer they got to the parade, the harder it was to see it. Then suddenly it was gone. The strange parade had vanished.

But the great stone pyramid was still there, towering above them.

Panting, Jack looked around.

What had happened? Where were the people? The oxen? The gold box? The cat?

"They're gone," said Annie.

"Where did they go?" said Jack.

"Maybe they were ghosts," said Annie.

"Don't be silly. There's no such thing as ghosts," said Jack. "It must have been a mirage."

"A what?"

"Mirage. It happens in the desert all the time," said Jack. "It looks like something's there. But it just turns out to be the sunlight reflecting through heat."

"How could sunlight look like people, a mummy box, and a bunch of cows?" said Annie.

Jack frowned.

"Ghosts," she said.

"No way," said Jack.

"Look!" Annie pointed at the pyramid.

Near the base was the sleek black cat. He was standing alone. He was staring at Jack and Annie.

"*He's* no mirage," said Annie.

The cat started to slink away. He walked along the side of the pyramid and slid around a corner.

"Where's he going?" said Jack.

"Let's find out," said Annie.

Mary Pope Osborne

They dashed around the corner just in time
to see the cat disappear through a hole in the
pyramid wall.

CHAPTER THREE

IT'S ALIVE!

"Where did he go?" said Jack.

He and Annie peeked through the hole in the wall. They saw a long hallway. Burning torches lit the walls. Dark shadows loomed.

"Let's go in," said Annie.

"Wait," said Jack.

He pulled out the Egypt book and turned to the section on pyramids.

He read the caption aloud:

Pyramids were sometimes called Houses of the Dead. They were nearly all solid stone, except for the burial chambers deep inside.

"Wow. Let's go there. To the burial chambers," said Annie. "I bet a mummy's there."

Jack took a deep breath.

Then he stepped out of the hot, bright sunlight into the cool, dark pyramid.

'The hallway was silent.

Floor, ceiling, walls—everything was stone. The floor slanted up from where they stood.

"We have to go farther inside," said Annie.

"Right," said Jack. "But stay close behind me. Don't talk. Don't—"

"Go! Just go!" said Annie. She gave him a little push.

Jack started up the slanting floor of the hallway.

Mummies in the Morning

Where was the cat?

The hallway went on and on.

"Wait," said Jack. "I want to look at the book."

He opened the Egypt book again. He held it below a torch on the wall. The book showed a drawing of the inside of the pyramid.

"The burial chamber is in the middle of the pyramid. See?" Jack said. He pointed to the drawing. "It should be straight ahead."

Jack tucked the book under his arm. Then he and Annie headed deeper into the pyramid.

Soon the floor became flat. The air felt different—musty and stale.

Jack opened the book again. "I think we're almost at the burial chamber. See the picture? The hallway slants up. Then it gets flat. Then you come to the chamber. See, look—"

"*Eee-eee!*" A strange cry shot through the pyramid.

Mary Pope Osborne

Jack dropped the Egypt book.

Out of the shadows flew a white figure.

It swooshed toward them!

A mummy! Jack thought.

"It's alive!" Annie shouted.

CHAPTER FOUR

BACK FROM THE DEAD

Jack pulled Annie down.

The white figure moved swiftly past them, then disappeared into the shadows.

"A mummy," said Annie. "Back from the dead!"

"F-forget it," stammered Jack. "That's impossible." He picked up the Egypt book.

"What's this?" said Annie. She lifted something from the floor. "Look. The mummy dropped this thing."

It was a gold stick about a foot long. A dog's head was carved on one end.

"It looks like a scepter," said Jack.

"What's that?" asked Annie.

"It's a thing kings and queens carry," said Jack. "It means they have power over the people."

"Come back, mummy!" Annie called. "We found your scepter. Come back! We want to help you!"

"Shush!" said Jack. "Are you nuts?"

"But the mummy—"

"That was no mummy," said Jack. "It was a person. A real person."

"What kind of person would be inside a pyramid?" asked Annie.

"I don't know," said Jack. "Maybe the book can help us."

He flipped through the book. At last he found a picture of a person in a pyramid. He read:

Mummies in the Morning

Tomb robbers often stole the treasure buried with mummies. False passages were sometimes built to stop the robbers.

Jack closed the book. "Not a mummy," he said. "Just a tomb robber."

"Yikes. A tomb robber?" said Annie.

"Yeah, a robber who steals stuff from tombs," said Jack.

"What if the robber comes back?" said Annie. "We'd better leave."

"Right," said Jack. "But first I want to write something down."

He put the Egypt book into his pack. He pulled out his notebook and pencil.

He started writing in his notebook:

tomb robber

"Jack—" said Annie.

"Just a second," said Jack. He kept writing:

tomb robber tried to steal

"Jack! Look!" said Annie.

Jack felt a *whoosh* of cold air. He looked up. A wave of terror shot through him.

Another figure was moving slowly toward them.

It wasn't a tomb robber. It was a lady. A beautiful Egyptian lady.

The lady wore flowers in her black hair. Her long white dress had many tiny pleats. Her gold jewelry glittered.

"Here, Jack," Annie whispered. "Give her this." She handed him the gold scepter.

The Egyptian lady stopped in front of them.

Jack held out the scepter. His hand was trembling.

Mummies in the Morning

He gasped. The scepter passed right through the lady's hand.

She was made of air.

CHAPTER FIVE

THE GHOST-QUEEN

"A ghost," Annie whispered.

Jack could only stare in horror.

The ghost began to speak. She spoke in a hollow, echoing voice.

"I am Hutepi," she said. "Queen of the Nile. Have you come to help me?"

Jack still couldn't speak.

"Yes," said Annie.

"For a thousand years," said the ghost-queen, "I have waited for help."

Jack's heart was pounding so hard he thought he might faint.

"Someone must find my Book of the Dead," she said. "I need it to go on to the Next Life."

"Why do you need the Book of the Dead?" asked Annie. She didn't sound scared at all.

"It will tell me the magic spells I need to get through the Underworld," said the ghost-queen.

"The Underworld?" said Annie.

"Before I journey on to the Next Life, I must pass through the horrors of the Underworld."

"What kinds of horrors?" Annie asked.

"Poisonous snakes," said the ghost-queen. "Lakes of fire. Monsters. Demons."

"Oh." Annie stepped closer to Jack.

"My brother hid the Book of the Dead so tomb robbers would not steal it," said the ghost-queen. "Then he carved this secret message on the wall, telling me how to find it." She pointed to the wall.

Jack was still in shock. He couldn't move.

"Where?" Annie asked her. "Here?" She squinted at the wall. "What do these tiny pictures mean?"

The ghost-queen smiled sadly. "Alas, my brother forgot my strange problem. I cannot see clearly that which is close to my eyes. I have not been able to read his message for thousands of years."

"Oh, that's not strange," said Annie. "Jack has the same problem. That's why he wears glasses."

Mummies in the Morning

The ghost-queen stared in wonder at Jack.
"Jack, lend her your glasses," said Annie.
Jack took his glasses off his nose. He held
them out to the ghost-queen.

She backed away from him. "I cannot wear your glasses, Jack," she said. "As you can see, I am made of air."

"Oh, I forgot," said Annie.

"But perhaps you will describe the hieroglyphs on this wall," said the ghost-queen.

"Hi-ro-who?" said Annie.

"Hieroglyphs!" said Jack, finally finding his voice. "It's the ancient Egyptian way of writing. It's like writing with pictures."

The ghost-queen smiled at him. "Thank you, Jack," she said.

Jack smiled back at her. He put his glasses on. Then he stepped toward the wall and took a good long look.

"Oh, man," he whispered.

CHAPTER SIX

THE WRITING ON THE WALL

Jack and Annie squinted at the pyramid wall.

A series of tiny pictures was carved into the stone.

"There are four pictures here," Jack told the ghost-queen.

"Describe them to me, Jack. One at a time, please," she said.

Jack studied the first picture.

"Okay," he said. "The first one is like this."
He made a zigzag in the air with his finger.

"Like stairs?" asked the ghost-queen.

"Yes, stairs!" said Jack. "Just like stairs."

She nodded. *That was easy enough,* Jack
thought. He studied the second picture.

"The second one has a long box on the bottom," he said. He drew it in the air.

The ghost-queen looked puzzled.

"With three things on top. Like this," said
Annie. She drew squiggly lines in the air.

The ghost-queen still seemed puzzled.

"Like a hat," said Jack.

"Hat?" said the ghost-queen.

"No. More like a boat," said Annie.

"Boat?" said the ghost-queen. She sounded excited. "Boat?"

Jack took another look at the wall.

"Yes. It could be a boat," he said.

The ghost-queen looked very happy. She smiled. "Yes. Of course," she said.

Jack and Annie studied the next picture.

"The third one is like a thing that holds flowers," said Annie.

"Or a thing that holds water," said Jack.

"Like a jug?" asked the ghost-queen.

"Exactly," said Jack.

"Yes. A jug," said Annie.

Jack and Annie studied the last picture.

"And the last one looks like a pole that droops," said Annie.

"Like a curved stick," said Jack. "But one side is shorter than the other."

The ghost-queen looked puzzled again.

"Wait," said Jack. "I'll draw it in my notebook. Big! So you can see it."

Jack put down the scepter and got out his pencil. He drew the hieroglyph.

"A folded cloth," said the ghost-queen.

"Really?" said Jack.

"Yes. That is the hieroglyph for a folded cloth," said the ghost-queen.

"Oh. Okay," said Jack.

He looked at the fourth hieroglyph again.

He still couldn't see the folded cloth. Maybe it was like a towel hanging over a bathroom rod.

"So that's all of them," said Annie. She pointed at each picture. "Stairs. Boat. Jug. Folded cloth."

Jack wrote the words in his notebook.

stairs = ⬜   jug = 🝮

boat = 〰️   cloth = ⁊

"So what does the message mean?" he asked the ghost-queen.

"Come," she said. She held out her hand. "Come to my burial chambers."

And she floated away.

CHAPTER SEVEN

THE SCROLL

Jack put the scepter and his notebook and pencil into his pack. The ghost-queen seemed so kind and gentle. He wasn't afraid of her at all anymore.

Jack and Annie followed her deeper into the pyramid. Finally they came to some stairs.

"The STAIRS!" said Jack and Annie together.

The ghost-queen floated up the stairs.

Jack and Annie followed.

The ghost-queen floated right through a wooden door.

Jack and Annie pushed on the door. It opened slowly. They stepped into a cold, drafty room.

The ghost-queen was nowhere in sight.

Dim torchlight lit the huge room. It had a very high ceiling. On one side was a pile of tables, chairs, and musical instruments.

On the other side of the room was a small wooden boat.

"The BOAT!" said Jack.

"What's it doing inside Queen Hutepi's pyramid?" asked Annie.

"Maybe it's supposed to carry her to the Next Life," said Jack.

Jack and Annie went over to the boat. They looked inside it.

The boat was filled with many things—gold plates, painted cups, jeweled goblets, woven baskets, jewelry with blue stones, and small wooden statues.

Mummies in the Morning

"Look!" said Jack. He reached into the boat and lifted out a clay jug.

"The JUG!" said Annie.

Jack looked inside the jug. "Something's in here," he said.

"What is it?" asked Annie.

Jack felt inside the jug. "It feels like a big napkin," he said.

"The FOLDED CLOTH!" said Annie.

Jack reached into the jug and pulled out the folded cloth. It was wrapped around an ancient-looking scroll.

Jack slowly unrolled the scroll. It was covered with wonderful hieroglyphs.

"The Book of the Dead!" whispered Annie. "We found it."

"Oh, man." Jack traced his finger over the scroll. It felt like very old paper.

"Queen Hutepi!" called Annie. "We have it! We found your Book of the Dead!"

Mary Pope Osborne

Silence. "Queen Hutepi!"

A door on the other side of the chamber creaked open.

"Maybe she's in there," said Annie.

Jack's heart was pounding. Cold air was coming through the open doorway.

"Come on," said Annie.

"Wait—"

"No," said Annie. "She's waited thousands of years for her book. Don't make her wait anymore."

Jack put the ancient scroll into his backpack. Then he and Annie slowly started to cross the drafty room.

They came to the open door. Annie went through first.

"Hurry, Jack!" she said.

Jack stepped into the other room. It was nearly bare, except for a long gold box. The box was open. Its cover was on the floor.

"Queen Hutepi?" called Annie.

Silence.

"We found it," said Annie. "Your Book of the Dead."

Mummies in the Morning

There was still no sign of the ghost-queen.

The gold box glowed.

Jack could barely breathe. "Let's leave the scroll on the floor and go," he said.

"No. I think we should leave it in there," said Annie. She pointed to the gold box.

"No," said Jack.

"Don't be afraid," said Annie. "Come on."

Annie took Jack by the arm. They walked together across the room to the glowing gold box.

They stopped in front of the box and peered inside.

CHAPTER EIGHT

THE MUMMY

A real mummy, Jack thought.

Bandages were still wrapped around the mummy's skull, but most of the bandages had fallen away from the face.

It was Hutepi. Queen of the Nile.

Hutepi's mummy wasn't beautiful. It had broken teeth, little wrinkled ears, and a squashed nose. Its flesh had withered. Its eyes were hollow sockets.

The rotting bandages on the mummy's body were coming off. Jack could see bones.

Mummies in the Morning

"Oh, gross!" cried Annie. "Let's go!"

"No," said Jack. "It's interesting."

"Forget it!" said Annie. She started out of the room.

"Wait, Annie."

"Come on, Jack. Hurry!" cried Annie. She was standing by the door.

Jack pulled out the Egypt book and flipped to a picture of a mummy. He read aloud:

Ancient Egyptians tried to protect the body so it would last forever. First it was dried out with salt.

"Ugh, stop!" said Annie.

"Listen," said Jack. He kept reading:

Next it was covered with oil. Then it was wrapped tightly in bandages. The brain was removed by—

 45

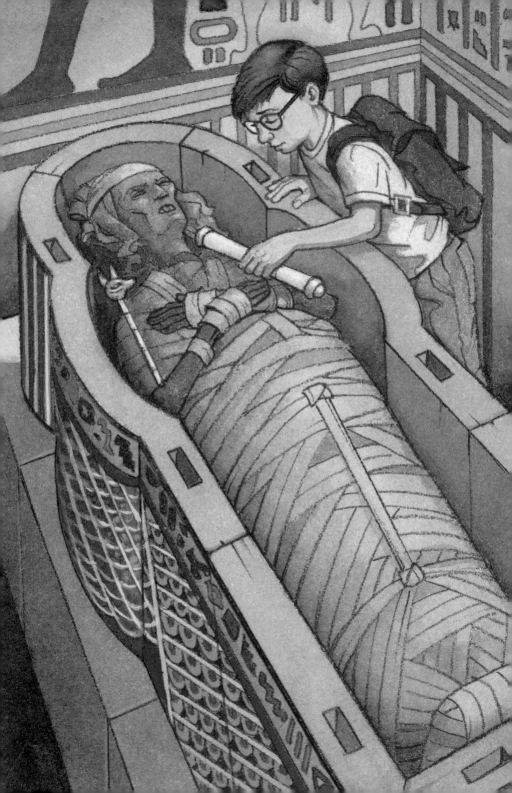

Mummies in the Morning

"Yuck! Stop!" cried Annie. "Good-bye!" She dashed out of the room.

"Annie!" called Jack. "We have to give her the Book of the Dead!"

But Annie was gone.

Jack reached into his pack. He pulled out the scroll and the scepter. He put them next to the mummy's skull.

Was it just his imagination? Or did a deep sigh seem to shudder throughout the room? Did the mummy's face grow calmer?

Jack held his breath as he backed out of the mummy room. He hurried through the boat room and headed down the stairs.

At the bottom of the stairs, Jack heaved his own sigh, a sigh of relief.

He looked down the hallway. It was empty.

"Hey! Annie! Where are you?" he said.

No answer.

Where in the world was Annie?

Jack started down the hallway. "Annie!" he called.

Had she run out of the pyramid? Was she already outside?

"Annie!"

"Help, Jack!" came a cry. The voice sounded far away.

It was Annie! Where was she?

"Help, Jack!"

"Annie!"

Jack started to run along the shadowy hallway.

"Help, Jack!" Her cry seemed fainter.

Jack stopped.

He was running *away* from her voice.

"Annie!" he called. He went back toward the burial chambers.

"Jack!" Her voice was louder.

"JACK!"

Jack climbed the stairs. He went back into the boat room. He looked around at the furniture, the musical instruments, and the boat.

Then he saw it. There was another door! It was right next to the door he had just come through!

The other door was open.

Jack dashed through it. He found himself at the top of some stairs.

They were just like the stairs outside the other door.

He went down the stairs and into a hallway. It was lit by torches on the wall.

It was just like the other hallway.

"Annie!" he called.

"Jack!"

"Annie!"

"Jack!" Annie was running through the hallway toward him. She crashed into him.

"I was lost!" she cried.

"I think this is one of those false passages built to fool the tomb robbers," said Jack.

"A false passage?" said Annie, panting.

"Yeah, it looks just like the other hallway," said Jack. "We have to go back into the boat room and out the right door."

Just then they heard a creaking noise.

Jack and Annie turned around. They looked up the stairs.

They watched in horror as the door slowly creaked shut.

A deep sound rumbled in the distance and all the torches went out.

CHAPTER NINE

FOLLOW THE LEADER

It was pitch-dark.

"What happened?" asked Annie.

"I don't know. Something weird," said Jack. "We have to get out of here fast. Push against the door."

"Good idea," said Annie in a small voice.

They felt their way through the darkness to the top of the stairs.

"Don't worry. Everything's going to be okay," said Jack. He was trying to stay calm.

"Of course," said Annie.

They leaned against the wooden door and pushed.

It wouldn't budge.

They pushed harder.

It was no use.

Jack took a deep breath. It was getting harder to breathe and harder to stay calm.

"What can we do?" asked Annie.

"Just . . . just rest a minute," said Jack, panting. His heart was pounding as he tried to see through the darkness.

"Maybe we should start down the hall," Annie said. "Maybe we'll eventually come to . . . to an exit."

Jack wasn't sure about that, but they had no choice.

"Okay, come on," he said. "Feel the wall."

Jack felt the stone wall as he climbed slowly down the stairs. Annie followed.

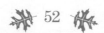

Mummies in the Morning

Jack started down the dark hallway. It was impossible to see anything. But he kept going, taking one step at a time, moving his hands along the wall.

Jack went around a corner. He went around another corner. He came to some stairs. He climbed up. Annie followed.

There was a door. Jack pushed against it. Annie pushed, too. This door wouldn't budge, either. Or was it the same door?

Jack and Annie stopped pushing. It was no use. They were trapped.

Annie took Jack's hand in the dark. She squeezed it.

They stood together at the top of the stairs, listening to the silence.

"Meow."

"Oh, man," Jack whispered.

"He's back!" said Annie.

"Meow."

"Follow him!" cried Jack. "He's going away from us."

Mummies in the Morning

Jack and Annie started down the dark hallway, following the cat's meow. Hands against
the wall, they stumbled through the darkness.
"Meow."

Jack and Annie kept following the sound, all the way through the winding hallway.

They went around one corner, then another, and another. . . .

Finally they saw a light at the end of the tunnel. They rushed forward—out into the bright sunlight.

"Yay!" Annie shouted.

But Jack was thinking. "Annie," he said. "How did we get out of the false passage?"

"The cat," said Annie.

"But how could the cat do it?" asked Jack.

"Magic," said Annie.

Jack frowned. "But—"

"Look!" said Annie. She pointed.

The cat was bounding away, over the sand.

"Thank you!" called Annie.

"Thanks!" Jack shouted at the cat.

The cat's black tail waved. Then the cat disappeared in the shimmering waves of heat.

Jack looked toward the palm trees. The magic tree house sat like a bird's nest at the top of one.

"Time to go home," Jack said.

Jack and Annie set off for the palm trees. It was a long, hot walk.

At last Annie grabbed the rope ladder. Jack followed.

Once they were inside the tree house, Jack reached for the book about Pennsylvania.

Suddenly he heard a rumbling sound. It was the same sound he had heard in the pyramid.

"Look!" Annie said, pointing out the window.

Jack looked.

A boat was beside the pyramid. It was gliding over the sand like a boat sailing over the sea.

Then the boat faded away into the distance.

Was it just a mirage? Or was the ghost-queen finally on her way to the Next Life?

"Home, Jack," whispered Annie.

Jack opened the Pennsylvania book.

He pointed to the picture of Frog Creek.

"I wish we could go home," he said.

The wind began to blow.

The tree house started to spin.

It spun faster and faster.

Then everything was still.

Absolutely still.

CHAPTER TEN

ANOTHER CLUE

Late-morning sunlight shone through the tree house window. Shadows danced on the walls and ceiling.

Jack took a deep breath. The tree house was back in the Frog Creek woods.

"I wonder what Mom's making for lunch," said Annie. She was looking out the window.

Jack smiled. Lunch. Mom. Home. It all sounded so real, so calm and safe.

"I hope it's peanut butter and jelly sand-wiches," he said.

"Boy, this place is a mess," said Annie. "We'd better make it neater in case M comes back."

Jack had almost forgotten about M.

Will we ever meet M? Jack wondered. *The person who seems to own all the books in the tree house?*

"Let's put the Egypt book on the bottom of the pile," said Annie.

"Good idea," said Jack. He needed a rest before he visited any more ancient tombs.

"Let's put the dinosaur book on top of the Egypt book," said Annie.

"Yeah, good," said Jack. He needed a *long* rest before he visited another Tyrannosaurus rex.

"The castle book can go on the very top of the pile," said Annie.

Jack nodded and smiled. He liked thinking about the knight on the cover of the castle book.

He felt as if the knight was his friend.

"Jack," said Annie. "Look!" She was point-ing at the wooden floor.

"What is it?" he asked.

"You have to see for yourself."

Jack walked to Annie and looked at the floor. He didn't see anything.

"Turn your head a little," said Annie. "You have to catch the light just right."

Jack tipped his head to one side. Something was shining on the floor.

He tipped his head a bit more. It came into focus.

It was the letter M! It shimmered in the sunlight.

This absolutely proved the tree house belonged to M. There was no doubt about it.

Jack touched the M with his finger. His skin tingled.

The leaves trembled. The wind picked up.

"Let's go home now," Jack said.

Jack grabbed his backpack. Then he and Annie climbed down the ladder.

As they stood on the ground below the tree house, Jack heard a sound in the bushes.

"Who's there?" he called.

The woods grew still.

"I'm going to bring the medallion back soon," Jack said loudly. "And the bookmark, too. Both of them. Tomorrow!"

"Who are you talking to?" asked Annie.

"I feel like M is nearby," Jack whispered.

Annie's eyes grew wide. "Should we look for M?"

But just then their mother's voice came from the distance. "Ja-ack! An-nie!"

Jack and Annie looked around at the trees. Then they looked at each other.

"Tomorrow," they said together.

They took off, running out of the woods.

They ran down their street.

They ran across their yard.

They ran into their house.

They ran into their kitchen.

They ran right into their mom.

She was making peanut butter and jelly sandwiches.

Turn the page for mummy and pyramid facts from the Magic Tree House Fact Tracker: *Mummies and Pyramids*

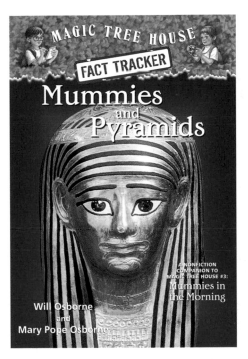

The Nile River

The Nile gave the ancient Egyptians water for drinking and bathing. Egyptian fishermen caught many kinds of fish in the Nile. Hunters hunted wild birds along its banks. Boats sailed up and down the Nile, carrying people and goods.

Temples

The Egyptians built great temples for their most important gods and goddesses. Inside the temples were sacred statues. Priests at the temples cared for the statues. They washed and dressed them. They even served them meals!

THOTH (THOTH or TOTE)

Thoth was the moon god. Egyptians believed Thoth gave them the gift of writing. He was also the god of medicine and mathematics. He was sometimes shown as a baboon. He was also shown as a man with the head of a bird.

BES (BES)

Bes was one of the Egyptians' favorite gods. He was short, chubby, and happy. He had a lion's ears and tail—and the body and face of a man. Bes brought joy and good luck to families. He protected the whole household.

Building the Pyramids

It took many years to build a pyramid. It also took thousands of workers.

Egyptologists think the workers used wooden rollers to move giant stones across the desert. Some of these stones weighed over 4,000 pounds!

No one really knows exactly how the workers put the giant stones in place. Most Egyptologists think they built large ramps to raise the stones up the sides of

the pyramid. When the pyramid was fin-
ished, the ramps were torn down.

Many people think the work on the
pyramids was done by slaves. This is not
true. Almost all the work was done by
farmers during the flood season.

The farmers were paid to help build the
pyramids. But most of them worked for a
reason more important than money. They
believed building the pyramids would help
them get to the Next Life when they died.

THE MAGIC TREE HOUSE® SERIES

Mary Pope Osborne has written more than a hundred books for children, including novels, biographies, picture books, and retellings of mythology and folktales. Soon after she started writing the Magic Tree House series over twenty years ago, Mary began visiting schools and libraries all over the country to meet with teachers, parents, and children. In 2012, as a twentieth-anniversary gift to all the educators who've been so supportive of the series, she created the Magic Tree House Classroom Adventures Program at MTHClassroomAdventures.org, a free resource for teachers who use Jack and Annie's adventures to energize their curriculum. Mary invites teachers to use the program to inspire a lifelong passion for reading and learning.

ABOUT
THE ILLUSTRATOR

Sal Murdocca is best known as the illustrator of the *New York Times* bestselling Magic Tree House series. Sal has authored ten children's books and has illustrated numerous picture books and series. Before turning to children's books, he worked in advertising and magazine illustration, and also taught writing and illustration at Parsons School of Design. Sal is from Brooklyn, New York. He attended the High School of Art and Design and studied at the Art Students League in New York City. He and his wife, the artist Nancy Caravan, divide their time between their home in upstate New York and their house in the south of France.

NANCY CARAVAN

AUTHOR'S ACKNOWLEDGMENTS

I would like to thank all the readers, parents, and teachers who have inspired me to keep writing the Magic Tree House series for over twenty years.

And of course, I'm forever grateful to my husband, Will Osborne, and my sister, Natalie Pope Boyce, for cowriting the Magic Tree House Fact Tracker series—and to Will, Randy Courts, and Jenny Laird for creating live shows to expand the series.

I also give great thanks to the team who has worked together and journeyed with me on all of Jack and Annie's adventures: my agent, Gail Hochman; my editor, Mallory Loehr; art director Cathy Goldsmith; and illustrator Sal Murdocca. *Mummies in the Morning* wouldn't have come into existence without this team. Nor would the more than fifty books that came after—and the others yet to come. As Annie says to Jack in *Magic Tree House: The Musical:* "None of this would be much fun if we were doing it by ourselves."